The Tiny Christmas Elf

Written by Sharon Peters

Illustrated by Julie Durrell

Troll Associates

Library of Congress Cataloging in Publication Data

Peters, Sharon.
    The tiny Christmas elf.

    Summary: The Christmas elf is Santa's special
helper, assisting him in his holiday tasks and helping
him have a merry Christmas himself.
    [1. Fairies—Fiction. 2. Santa Claus—Fiction.
3. Christmas—Fiction] 1. Durrell, Julie, ill.
II. Title.
PZ7.P44183Ti   1987   [E]   86-30849
ISBN 0-8167-0988-2 (lib. bdg.)
ISBN 0-8167-0989-0 (pbk.)

You know that Santa has a red cap
and coat.

You know he has eight reindeer . . .

and a sled full of presents.

But do you know what else Santa
has?

He has a helper.

The Christmas elf is Santa's helper.

The Christmas elf is tiny.

He has a tiny red cap and coat.

He has eight tiny reindeer . . .

and a sled full of tiny presents.

The Christmas elf helps Santa bring presents.

He can fit in tiny places.

So that everyone can have a merry
Christmas.

Santa can go here.

And Santa can go there.

But can Santa go here? No!

Santa needs help.

The Christmas elf can help Santa.

He can go here.

He can fit here.

When Santa needs help, the
Christmas elf is there.

He brings tiny presents.

He can fit in tiny places.

So that everyone can have a merry Christmas.

But do you know what else the
Christmas elf does?

He helps Santa have a merry Christmas.

The Christmas elf brings Santa a present, too.

Merry Christmas, Santa!